Love, Life and Laws

Love, Life and Laws

DANIA MEHDI

First published by
Papertowns Publishers
72, Vishwanath Dham Colony,
Niwaru Road, Jhotwara,
Jaipur, 302012

Love, Life and Laws
Copyright © Dania Mehdi, 2021

ISBN Print Book - 978-93-91228-84-2

Cover Design by Narendra Singh
narendra@thebookoholics.com

AUTHOR BIO

Lucknow based Dania Mehdi is a Nineteen years old writer and an author of a new book 'Love, Life and Laws.' A class XII intermediate student of City Montessori School Rajajipuram Campus-1, Dania has spent her last few years reading and writing stories and giving her characters palpable spark!

DEDICATION

Writing is not only about imagination; it's also about surroundings, seeing things happening by your side. It gives you a lot of ideas. I started writing when I was in class X. I always carried a diary with me and used to write in my free time.

No one was aware of my writing, and I was also quite apprehensive about it. One day, by chance, my friends read my diary and were very happy about my hidden talent, and they motivated me a lot.

I was scared as I used to think how my family and others are going to react. I stopped writing for two years, thinking people would laugh at my write-ups. Then in class XII, while giving the English Language exam, I attempted a story writing question where I wrote a story (Passion). My English teacher, Mrs. Lama Chandra Nigam, one of the best English teachers of my life, appreciated my work in front of everyone and told that my story brought tears to her eyes. I was overwhelmed, and I decided to take writing seriously. The same day, I went to my mother, an English teacher, and told her that I am into writing and asked her if she would like to read my stories. I made her read one of my stories, 'HER,' and then I got an unexpected reaction from her and my family. Everyone was so happy, and from there, they encouraged me a lot and motivated me to write more.

In the end, it's a big thank you to Lama ma'am, my family, and my friends.

ACKNOWLEDGEMENT

I would like to acknowledge, with gratitude, the support and love of my family-

My mother, Mrs. Maryam Imam, encouraged me the most and helped me throughout.

My father, Mr. Abid Mehdi, for supporting me.

My Fammi, Ms. Farah Imam, and my brother, Ali, for motivating me.

I would also like to thank my friends Riddhi Saini and Aanshi Pal for always being by my side and correcting me whenever I go wrong.

They prove the quote, "Friends like family and family like friends."

CONTENTS

"Her"

It was 2:30 pm. The last bell of the day rang, and the school got over. All the other students had left, except her. She was still waiting for her teacher to come and teach her after school. Unfortunately, all the teachers were busy in a meeting, and she sat in the hall waiting for them to come out. It was now 3 pm, and she was staying. No one else had been there all this while. One minute she was all alone in the hall, and then suddenly, he appeared before her and sat in the chair next to her. He whispered, "I want to tell you that I love you. I want to grow old with you, and you mean the world to me. I don't know whether you will say yes or no to that, but remember, you are my life." He kissed her forehead and waited for an answer.

Her eyes filled with tears. She was amazed by his gesture. She was so mesmerized by his words that she was not able to utter a single word. In her heart, she said 'yes' a thousand times. But now, when in **real-time** the moment had arrived, and she was going to say 'Yes, I love you too,' the chair fell, and she was shocked to see an empty hall.

Yes, the stupid girl was once again daydreaming about him. It was all because she loved him a lot. He loved her too. The only problem was, for him, 'Her' was someone else.

"*Passion*"

With a look of supreme confidence, she walked up the stage. Her big, beautiful, bright, and confident smile made me happy. Today Avantika danced like a peacock. She was dancing like no one was seeing her.

I knew Avantika since my childhood. I was five years old when she and her family had shifted to our neighbourhood. Since then, we had become good friends. We went to the same school till class X, but later she had changed her school. We had always been more like sisters.

Avantika was extremely talented. She learned classical dance from her Guru Ji for ten years. From the age of five, she was learning dance, and now she was a professional dancer. She won many awards for her dance. Sometimes we used to sit and stare at her and think how a person can dance so effortlessly. She was passionate and obsessed with her dance, but as it is said, nothing lasts forever. Things changed and changed like hell.

She was crossing the road when a drunk driver hit her with his car. People took her to the hospital, but it was already too late. When I reached the hospital and enquired, doctors told me that they had no option left, and they had to amputate her right leg as some nerves have been damaged. I was shocked as I knew that she would not be able to handle this trauma. There is no bigger curse for a dancer than losing a leg. When she saw me entering the room, she said nothing as if she had just lost all her hopes and confidence.

After six months, doctors fixed an artificial leg for her, and they permitted her to dance. However, she said nothing and just left. Whenever she tried dancing, she would fall and feel miserable all over again, as if she had just lost all her self-confidence and happiness. I took her to the therapist after seeing her condition. Every week I used to go with her. Slowly she started smiling and accepted the truth of her life. She used to dance and fall, but she never gave up, and I was happy seeing her happy.

One day in the afternoon, when I was sleeping, I got a call. It was Avantika. I was shocked as it was very unusual of her to call me. She would never call me, as we had a habit of texting each other. The moment I answered the call, she said," Immediately come to the address I have sent you." And she kept the phone. I was scared. I immediately rushed to the location she had sent me. It turned out to be a hall. It was filled with more than two hundred people sitting. And on the stage, there was Avantika. She was standing alone and looking like a doll. She walked onto the stage with supreme confidence while giving me a big smile and then started dancing. The crowd was going crazy seeing her dance. People were clapping and appreciating her. Seeing this, my eyes filled with tears, and I went on the stage and hugged her. Avantika's belief in herself changed every pain into gain, and now she is a dance teacher in an institute.

"The wedding day"

Finally, the day had come when Samayra was getting married to Ankush. The man she loved the most and with whom she was in a relationship for the last ten years. She was getting ready, and she definitely was the most beautiful bride there ever could be. Her beauty made a simple red saree look royal. Her mother came inside the room and got tears in her eyes just seeing her. She was happy to see her daughter as a bride. They both exchanged a smile, and the beauty of the bond between a mother and her daughter was flawlessly visible in that one smile. Suddenly someone said from behind, "Pandit Ji is calling Samayra, the groom has reached." She blushed and flickered, and her mother took her down. While walking down the stairs, she got nervous, but still, her eyes were finding him.

Ankush sitting near Pandit Ji, was utterly mesmerized after seeing Samayra. He gradually stood up and went near the stairs. He held her hand and took her to the mandap. They sat down, and she mumbled, "Looking damn hot" he looked at her and said, 'thanks,' and they both chuckled. After the jaimaala (exchanging of the garlands), Pandit Ji asked them to stand for the pheras (the ritual where the bride and groom circle the holy fire seven times).

Four pheras were completed. Pandit Ji then asked Samayra to come in the front. Suddenly she shrieked in pain and fainted. There was chaos all around the hall. Ankush took Samayra inside the room, and the family apologized and asked the guests to leave. The family was worried. Ankush was in the room with Samayra as she was still unconscious. The doctor came and checked her. He suggested the family take Samayra to the hospital for better treatment and few tests. He asked the family to stay strong and assured them that everything would be alright.

Ankush questioned the doctor about Samayra's condition and what had actually happened to her. Doctor asked him to wait for the reports.

The night was really dark for them, just like a nightmare that they wanted to end soon.

The following day Samayra gained her consciousness back and was lying on the hospital bed. Ankush entered the room with guilt in his eyes and asked her parents to go out of the room as he wanted to talk to her alone. Something was wrong, and Samayra could sense it, but then she ran and hugged him. Slowly, he pushed her away and handed over her test reports that stated she was diagnosed with melanoma (skin cancer). "I am sorry," he said. "Why are you sorry?" she asked.

"Sorry, as now I cannot marry you."

She just looked at his face and said nothing. "What is the need of getting married to you now? I cannot invest my time, money, emotions, and life in a girl who will die soon. If I had known this before, I would have never wasted my time on you." She was shattered. "But...but we love each other, Right???"

"What is love? Love can happen after an arranged marriage also. The main reason for getting married to someone is lifelong togetherness and, most importantly, kids. You are not even in a condition to give me my son."

As he was speaking slowly, tears started rolling out of her eyes. She completely broke down as she lost everything in a second.

"What about those ten years??? I loved you from the age of fifteen. I decided on my subjects according to you. You wanted to study science, so I also took science. You wanted to be a doctor, so I left my Law and did a Ph.D. My life always revolved around you, and it still does."

"Oh, please! That's your foolishness. I never asked you to do all of that. This Ishq, Pyaar, Mohabbat looks good only in stories, not in real life. Please, for God's sake, come out of your dream world."

"What about our future which we imagined together?" She asked while sobbing.

"Are you serious? Future with you? I don't even know if you are even going to see tomorrow's sunrise or not.

She had no words left with her. She sobbed, and he stood up and went out, leaving her alone in the hospital to die and never looked back at her again.

"The wedding day 2.0 (Twisted End)"

For sometimes, Samayra didn't say a word. The moment he was again going to say something, she stood and slapped him and said, "It was my mistake" she walked out of the room and saw a fifteen-year-old girl standing next to the window and listening in to their conversation. Samayra gave a smile to that girl and said, "Do not give the control of your life and emotions in the hands of others. Do what your heart says, not what the person in your heart asks you to do." And she left the hospital. These were her last words, and it was the last time people saw her.

No one knew that where Samayra was, not even her parents. She just left a message, "I am going, going to live my life to the fullest on my own terms. I want to explore myself before I die. Please do not call me. I will surely come back before my last breath."

She died. She died happily after experiencing life with a new version of herself.

Seven years passed. Everyone moved on. Ankush lived a happy life with his wife and a five-year-old son till that tragic incident. In a car accident, Ankush got injured and was unconscious for two days. The doctor told his wife that he was out of danger but unconscious due to the shock.

The following day screaming sounds started coming from his room. When his family and doctors entered the room, they were shocked as Ankush could not move his body. The doctors told his wife that a nerve got damaged because of the injury in his brain. He was now paralyzed and probably would never be normal again.

After a few months, his wife left him forever, saying that she couldn't stay with a man who could not afford to keep her physically, mentally, and financially happy. He begged her not to leave, but she didn't stop and took their son along with her.

Months passed, Ankush was left all alone in the hospital. No one visited him, not even a single person. The only thing he used to do on the hospital bed was to think about Samayra. The way he had left her in her last days. Slowly, due to the injury and heavy medications, his brain stopped working, and he died.

As it is said, Karma is a bitch. When it comes to hit, it hit below the belt. History repeated itself. Ankush received what he did. "There's a natural law of karma that vindictive people, who go out of their way to hurt others, will end up broke and alone."

"Destiny"

"Mummy, please abhi nahi. You know I am not interested in this. Right now, there are many other things in life for me to focus upon. My career, my book and more."

"Haan toh mai kahan keh rahi hu ki shaadi karle? Bas ladke se mil le ek baar. Kya pata,achcha lag jaaye."

"Par...."

"Par-var kuch nahi. I have fixed your meeting for today with him, and you have to go, and that's my order....aur haan, kuch acha sa pehan ke jaana."

As a good daughter, Payal agreed to what her mother had said and went to meet the guy. As soon as she entered the restaurant, she saw no one except the hotel staff. The manager came to her and asked, "Miss Payal Rastogi?"

"Yes," she replied. "This way, ma'am."

She asked the manager why the restaurant was empty. With a smile, he replied, "Your mother booked the whole restaurant for you." She didn't know what to say further.

Payal was looking her best today. She wore a sky blue chicken kurta with white embroidery, white pants and a beautiful blue and white dupatta. Her hair was open, a simple stroke of kajal was enhancing the beauty of her eyes, the nude pink lipstick on her lips resembled how simple she was, and her oxidized silver jhumkas were perfectly complimenting her looks. After five minutes, a man of about six feet entered the restaurant. He was wearing a black shirt with narrow grey pants and black shoes. The sleeves of his shirt were folded, and he was very hot and very good looking.

As soon as Payal saw him, she immediately said, "Akarsh? Hi, remember? Payal, Payal Rastogi. Same school and same batch in class XII."

Akarsh took a minute and then said, "Yaa, I mean wow! That's amazing. And quite funny too! Since we never talked in school, and today we are meeting like this."

They both sat. The waiter came to take the order. Payal immediately said, "I will be having an Americano, and now you may ask, sir."

"I'll be having a simple cappuccino."

The waiter took the order. After he left, Akarsh said, "You turned out to be a beautiful woman both in and out."

Payal looked at him with a sarcastic look. Akarsh said, "No, no wait, I mean you were beautiful that time also!"

"Ya, ya do not change it now. I know I was fat and ugly during those days."

"Listen, you were not. I mean, you were just chubby."

"Yaar, please, this chubby sounds so fake."

They both smiled and looked into the eyes of each other by the time their coffee arrived. Akarsh asked, "So tell me, what are you doing right now."

Payal replied, "I am unemployed".

He looked at her with confusion, so Payal clarified, "I mean, I am a writer trying to complete my book."

"That's wonderful. I didn't know that you were into writing." Payal smiled and asked, "What about you?" "Right now, I am the head of an interior designing company." "Wow, that sounds so good. Achcha, if you don't mind, can I ask you a question."

"Is that even a question? Of course, you can."

"Kya mai apne baal bandh lu?"

"What?"

"Yaa, I mean, I just hate open hair, but you know how mothers are. My mom said kisi se milne jaa rahi ho,dhang se jaao!"

Payal took out a rubber band and started tying up her hair. Akarsh was just staring at her and wondering how someone can be so elegantly beautiful.

"Payal, tell me something about your past relationships and the number of boyfriends you have had."

"Me? Let me think. I think it was with Faiz, Jaun, Javed and.." "Ok, ok, stop. Your list seems to be quite long!"

"Haha, no stupid. These are all the writers of my favourite books. Faiz Ahmed Faiz, Jaun Elia and Javed Akhtar Sahab. Frankly speaking, I was dating my books all these years. In fact, you must know that you are the first person I am meeting like this."

"I just don't believe this! You seem to be a very romantic person, and you didn't have any boyfriend?"

"I am romantic just for my write-ups, but in reality, as an individual, I am the most unromantic person. You tell me about yourself. How many girlfriends did you have"

"I had one, but we got separated, and from that day, my parents are searching for girls for me."

"Achcha toh koi mili?"

"Tumhe kya lagta hai? Milli hoti toh kya main yahan hota?" At this, they both looked at each other and laughed.

One hour passed while they talked about random things from food to GDP, animals to humans, movies to webseries and everything else they could think of.

It was already nine. Payal asked to take a leave, and Akarsh offered to drop her home. But she told him that she came by her car. Payal packed her stuff, bid goodbye to Akarsh, and started walking. Akarsh was still sitting. As soon as she reached the gate, Akarsh shouted, "Payal, will you marry me? Shadi karogi mujhse?"

She turned and asked, "Tum batao! will you be able to handle a girl who is the world's most unromantic soul?"

Akarsh stood up, walked and came near her and said, "Let's make a deal!"

"Deal? What deal?"

"You say 'yes' for the marriage, and I'll teach you how to be romantic, accepted?"

Payal chuckled softly, blushed and said, "Goodbye, Akarsh." He held her hand and pulled her towards himself. With his other hand, he reached to her hair and removed the hairband and let her beautiful long hair down while saying in her ears, "It's not goodbye. It's, see you soon 'to be Mrs Mehra'."

Payal looked into his eyes and softly said, "See you soon, Mr Mehra."

You don't meet people by accident; there is always a reason behind it. Who knew the classmates who were not close to each other, never spoke to each other would one day meet and fall in love like this. As it is said, *what is meant to be, will always find a way to be.*

"*An unwanted and unsaid goodbye!*"

He entered the room and inquired if everything was alright. The doctor asked him to sit and told him, "Because of the car accident, your wife Aarvi had some major injuries in her brain. We were happy that she came out of the coma, but we cannot say anything right now. Internal bleeding has started in her body. We have tried all the options to save your wife, but...."

"But what?"

"Your wife has hardly 24 hours." Karan was in a state of shock. He didn't know what to do. He had never imagined a life without Aarvi. He requested the doctor to allow him to take Aarvi home. At first, the doctor hesitated, but then he let him as he wanted Aarvi to spend her last few hours with her family.

Karan entered Aarvi's ward with tears in his eyes and a fake smile on his face. Aarvi immediately asked, "Is everything alright?"

"Yaa, the doctor has given you discharge. We are going home." Aarvi was very happy. She hugged him and said, "Finally, I will be getting rid of the hospital and this smell of medicine."

It was 3 pm. Karan and Aarvi were leaving the hospital. Karan was still in a state of shock, and Aarvi was speaking nonstop. Karan stopped the car in front of their house. It started to rain. As soon as Aarvi was going to step down, Karan held her hand and looked into her eyes and said, "Let's sit and enjoy this rain. Just you and me."

"Is something wrong? Is there anything you are hiding from me?"

"No"

"Then let me go. Everyone must be waiting for us."

"No, not now. It's been more than three months that we are sitting like this." Karan insisted.

"Karan please," she slowly removed her hand from his hand and opened the car's lock. The moment she was going to step down from the car, he played her favourite song, "Abhi na jaao chhodh kar, ki dil abhi bhara nahi...." She looked back, closed the door and said, "You very well know how to stop me."

With tears in his eyes, Karan said, " Toh phir ruk jaao na hamesha ke liye. Jaana zaroori hai kya?"

Aarvi replied, "Stop behaving like a child. Sirf ghar jaane ko keh rahi hu...Tumhara peechha itni jaldi thodi na chhodungi."

"And you, please stop acting like ke kuch hua hi nahi, and you don't know anything. The doctor told me that you know about your condition. Do you know that every minute, every second, I'm scared that I'll lose you and I won't be able to see you again." said Karan.

This was the first time Aarvi had seen Karan break down. With tears in her eyes, she hugged him. Both of them were crying like kids into each other's arms. Karan finally got a hold of his feelings and asked Aarvi to go home with him, but Aarvi did not say a single word. She was not moving. Karan made her sit on the seat and saw that Aarvi was not breathing. Karan was in a state of shock. Aarvi died in his arms. She took her last breath in the arms of the person she loved the most in this world. Karan never wanted to bid her goodbye and was not even able to.

"The horrifying day"

It was a day different from any other. It was three pm, and the sky had turned black. Black clouds were all around with thunder and lightning, and in few seconds, it started raining. The weather was turning into the worst it had ever been.

Agni, standing at the window seeing the changing weather, thought something was wrong. This bad weather was clearly a sign that something was going to happen, something wrong. Very wrong.

Agni was all alone in the house, and she was scared. She could feel the negativity all around her. Agni immediately called her husband on his phone, "Hello, hello Parth, where are you?"

"Who is this?" Someone replied from the opposite side.

"I'm Parth's wife. Where is he? This is his number, and who are you?"

"Ma'am, I'm senior inspector Yash. Due to the bad weather and heavy rain, a car and a truck met with an accident. The truck driver is dead, and the person who was driving the car is injured badly. Our team has taken him to the city hospital. We got this phone from the car."

After hearing this, Agni was shattered. She did not know what to do next. She wiped off her tears and rushed to the hospital. Midway, she called Priya, her sister, and told her everything. Priya asked her not to panic and said to her that she was also reaching the hospital.

Agni reached the hospital, where she saw Priya and her husband Abhinav already standing. They entered the hospital and asked the receptionist about the recent accident case. The receptionist asked them to go to the operation theatre on the fourth floor.

When they reached the fourth floor, they saw police standing near the operation theatre. The police started questioning them about the injured man. Agni was not in a condition to give answers, so they were talking to Abhinav. The officer asked him to confirm the number of the car which met with the accident, and he confirmed that it was Parth's car.

The doctors came out of the OT soon after and declared the patient to be dead. They told everyone that due to so many facial injuries, his face was not in a condition to be seen. Agni lost all her senses. She started crying and screaming. Priya was trying to handle her while Abhinav completed the formalities.

Suddenly Agni turned and saw Parth coming from across the floor. She ran and hugged him tightly. Abhinav and Priya could not believe their eyes. Agni was not able to stop her tears from rolling down. Parth calmed her down and told everyone that the person in the OT was his friend Akarsh. He said that his wife was in labour, and due to bad weather, he was not getting any cab, so he had borrowed Parth's car. By mistake, Parth had left his phone in the car. As soon as he saw the news on TV about the accident, he had rushed to the hospital.

It was a day different from any other, filled with drama, confusion, and tears. Agni was happy that it was not Parth, but she thought it could have been him.